EASY EATS

Grab-and-Go EATS

by Katrina Jorgensen

CAPSTONE PRESS
a capstone imprint

Dabble Lab is published by Capstone Press, an imprint of Capstone.
1710 Roe Crest Drive
North Mankato, Minnesota 56003
www.capstonepub.com

Library of Congress Cataloging-in-Publication Data is available on the Library of Congress website.
ISBN: 978-1-4966-8099-0 (hardcover)
ISBN: 978-1-4966-8106-5 (eBook PDF)

Summary: Kids and families are always on the run between school, sports, and extracurricular events. Time is short. Spend those spare seconds wisely by creating tasty, healthy meals and snacks that can be enjoyed on the go!

Image Credits
All photos by Capstone Studio: Karon Dubke

Design Elements: Shutterstock

Editorial Credits
Editor: Mari Bolte; Designer: Sarah Bennett; Media Researcher: Eric Gohl; Production Specialist: Katy LaVigne; Photo Stylist: Sarah Schuette

Printed and bound in the USA.
3342

Contents

Introduction

Make your next meal ahead of time. Then take it with you when you're out and about. Whether it's a school lunch, a between-activities-booster, or even just an after-school snack, we've got you covered. Most of these recipes can be prepared and stored in the fridge, freezer, or pantry for easy access on the way out the door. Simply reheat if needed and then toss in your lunch bag for later.

How to Read a Recipe

Before you start creating, it's important to read the recipe from beginning to end. This will help you avoid a cooking catastrophe!

Safe Kitchen Basics

Safety in the kitchen is the very first step. Make sure you begin with clean hands, tools, and surfaces. Any time you handle raw meat, wash your hands and any tools or surfaces the meat touched. Some of the recipes involve hot surfaces or sharp equipment. Have an adult nearby to help supervise and assist to keep you safe.

Never use hot or sharp things without an adult's permission.

Recipe Reading Checklist

- Do you have all the ingredients and tools?
- Do you understand the techniques listed in the directions?
- Do you have enough time to make the recipe?
- Have you read through the ingredients list thoroughly, in case you have dietary or allergy restrictions?
- Using metric tools? Here are conversions to make your recipe measure up.

Standard	Metric
1/4 teaspoon	1.25 grams or milliliters
1/2 teaspoon	2.5 g or mL
1 teaspoon	5 g or mL
1 tablespoon	15 g or mL
1/4 cup	57 g (dry) or 60 mL (liquid)
1/3 cup	75 g (dry) or 80 mL (liquid)
1/2 cup	114 g (dry) or 125 mL (liquid)
2/3 cup	150 g (dry) or 160 mL (liquid)
3/4 cup	170 g (dry) or 175 mL (liquid)
1 cup	227 g (dry) or 240 mL (liquid)
1 quart	950 mL

- All temperatures in this book are Fahrenheit. Use the chart here if you're cooking in Celsius.

Fahrenheit	Celsius
325°	160°
350°	180°
375°	190°
400°	200°
425°	220°
450°	230°

Sausage and Egg Breakfast Rolls

Looking for a high-protein, flavor-packed meal that's great for breakfast, lunch, or dinner? These handheld rolls are an all-in-one package full of fluffy eggs, creamy cheese, and tasty sausage.

Prep time: 20 minutes • Cook time: 15–20 minutes • Makes 6 rolls

Tip

To store, let the rolls cool completely. Then wrap tightly in plastic wrap. Freeze for up to 1 month. To warm, place a frozen roll on a baking sheet. Bake at 350 degrees for 15 minutes.

Ingredients

5 eggs

²/₃ cup milk

pinch salt

1 tablespoon butter

flour, for dusting

13-ounce (370-gram) package refrigerated pizza dough

¼ cup shredded cheddar cheese

6 fully cooked sausages, cut into bite-sized pieces

1 tablespoon butter, melted

pinch salt and pepper

Tools

medium bowl

measuring cups/spoons

whisk

spatula

nonstick skillet

rolling pin

pizza cutter

baking sheet lined with parchment paper

pastry brush

1. Ask an adult to preheat the oven to 350 degrees.

2. Crack the eggs into a bowl. Add the milk and salt, and whisk well. Set aside.

3. Place a large nonstick skillet on the stove. Ask the adult to heat to medium. Spread the butter around the pan with a spatula as it melts.

4. Pour the egg mixture into the pan. Cook for 30 seconds. The eggs will start to set and become firm. Use the spatula to push the edges of the eggs toward the center of the pan.

5. Continue pushing the eggs with the spatula until all the egg is cooked and there is no more liquid in the pan. Remove the pan from the heat and set aside.

6. Unroll the pizza dough onto a well-floured surface. Sprinkle more flour over the top of the dough. Use a rolling pin to flatten the dough into a rectangle about ¼-inch (0.6-centimeters) thick. Use a pizza cutter to cut the dough into 8 smaller rectangles.

7. Evenly spread the scrambled egg on each piece of dough. Sprinkle cheese and sausage

over the egg. Starting on a long side, roll the dough over the filling to make a cylinder shape. Place all rolls on the baking sheet. Brush the tops with butter and season with salt and pepper.

8. Bake for 15 to 20 minutes or until golden brown.

   Variation If you're egg-free, you can use tofu or mashed or roasted potatoes instead.

Snickerdoodle Overnight Oatmeal

Scrumptious cookie-flavored oatmeal for breakfast? No baking required?
We're sold! Fill these portable jars with sweet, cinnamon-y goodness,
and let them set overnight. The next morning, just grab and go!

Prep time: 5 minutes • inactive time: 10-12 hours (inactive) • Makes 1 serving

Ingredients

½ cup rolled old-fashioned oats

¼ teaspoon cinnamon

1 tablespoon brown sugar

½ cup milk

¼ cup vanilla yogurt

1 tablespoon chia seeds

¼ teaspoon vanilla extract

Tools

measuring cups/spoons

half-pint (250 mL) mason jar with lid

stirring spoon

1. Combine all of the ingredients in the mason jar. Stir until everything is totally smooth.

2. Replace the jar's lid. Then place the jar in the refrigerator overnight.

3. In the morning, open the jar and stir. Then add any toppings before you eat.

Variations Here are some suggestions to show off your Snickerdoodle Overnight Oatmeal even more. Top your finished oats with any of the below:

Apple-Cinnamon
½ apple, diced
2 tablespoons toasted walnuts or almonds

Cocoa Banana
1 tablespoon mini chocolate chips
½ sliced banana

Peach Upside Down Cake
½ peach, diced
2 tablespoons toasted pecans

Blueberry Muffin
¼ cup blueberries
¼ cup granola

Cubandillas

Cuban sandwiches are made with roast pork, sliced ham, Swiss cheese, and pickles. Then they're pressed until crispy on the outside and gooey on the inside. These quick quesadillas give you the same flavor with a fraction of the work. These can be eaten hot or cold wherever you may go.

Prep time: 15 minutes • Cook time: 10 minutes • Makes 2 quesadillas

Ingredients

4 6-inch (15-cm) flour tortillas

2 teaspoons yellow mustard

2 ounces (57 grams) thin-sliced Swiss cheese

2 ounces thin-sliced deli ham

2 ounces thin-sliced deli roast pork

4 sandwich-sliced dill pickles

cooking spray

Tools

cutting board

measuring cups/spoons

spatula

nonstick skillet

pizza cutter

1. Lay 2 tortillas on a cutting board.

2. Divide and spread mustard on each tortilla. Top with Swiss cheese, ham, pork, and pickles. Cover with the other 2 tortillas.

3. Place a nonstick skillet on the stove. Ask an adult to turn the heat to medium-low.

4. Spritz the skillet with cooking spray. Set a tortilla with toppings in the skillet. Then place a plain tortilla on top.

5. Cook for about 3 to 5 minutes. When the cheese is melted and the tortilla on the bottom starts to brown, carefully flip it over.

6. Cook another 3 minutes, or until it's golden brown.

7. Transfer to a cutting board. Then repeat steps 4–6 with the other quesadilla.

8. Use a pizza cutter to slice the quesadillas into triangles. Serve hot, or wrap up cooled quesadilla wedges and keep cold for future meals.

   Variations To make this vegetarian, swap your meats with ½ cup cooked black beans and ¼ cup sweet corn kernels.

   Making more than 2? Keep finished quesadillas warm in a 225-degree oven.

   To make this vegan, follow the vegetarian recipe, but use your favorite vegan cheese.

Taco Salad in a Jar

Taking tacos to go can be a messy situation. Turning them into a travel-ready salad, though, and you've changed the Tex-Mex game. Simply pack and store your salads. When you're ready to chow down, pour the container into a bowl for a fast, convenient, and tasty meal.

Prep time: 10 minutes • Cook time: 45 minutes (20 minutes inactive)
• Makes 2 salads

Ingredients

For the dressing:

½ cup plain Greek yogurt

½ cup ranch dressing

½ cup your favorite salsa

For the salad:

6 ounces (170 grams) boneless,
   skinless chicken breast

pinch salt/pepper

¼ teaspoon paprika

1 cup cooked black beans

1 cup corn kernels

1 cup grape tomatoes,
   cut in half

2 cups chopped romaine
   or iceberg lettuce

tortilla chips

Tools

small bowl

measuring cups/spoons

whisk

2 pint-sized (500 mL) jars
   with lids

small baking dish

cooking thermometer

cutting board

chef's knife

1. Ask an adult to preheat the oven to 450 degrees.

2. To make the dressing, combine the Greek yogurt, ranch dressing, and salsa in a small bowl. Whisk to combine. Carefully pour the dressing evenly into the jars. Set aside.

3. To prep the chicken, pour the olive oil in a small baking dish. Add the chicken and coat it in the oil. Sprinkle salt, pepper, and paprika on both sides.

4. Place the baking dish in the oven and bake for 20 to 25 minutes. Have the adult check for doneness. Cooked chicken should be at least 165 degrees in the center. It will no longer be pink inside.

5. Set the chicken on a cutting board. Ask the adult to cut the chicken into small pieces. Let the pieces cool for 20 minutes.

6. Build your salad! Divide the black beans, corn, and tomatoes between the 2 jars. Then add the chicken and the lettuce. Pack things in tightly. Finally, add a small handful of tortilla chips and seal the jar shut with the lid.

7. Place in the refrigerator for up to 5 days. To eat, open the jar and pour the salad into a bowl. Stir to mix, and enjoy!

   Variation Skip the chicken in favor of diced meatless chicken strips. If you're vegan, be sure to swap the Greek yogurt and ranch dressing with vegan varieties.

Turkey Pita Pocket

Pita is a special flatbread that comes from the Mediterranean and Middle East. It is cooked at a really high temperature. The moisture in the dough causes an air pocket to form inside each piece of bread. That pocket makes the perfect pouch to pack full of your favorite sandwich fillings.

Prep time: 5 minutes • Cook time: 0 minutes • Makes 2 pita sandwiches

Ingredients

For the sauce:

¼ cup plain Greek yogurt
¼ teaspoon garlic powder
¼ teaspoon dried dill weed
½ teaspoon fresh lemon juice
¼ cup grated cucumber
pinch salt/pepper

For the pita:

1 pita bread round
4 slices deli turkey
2 slices tomato
¼ cup baby spinach
4 slices cucumber

Tools

small bowl
measuring cups/spoons
grater
spoon
cutting board
knife
plastic wrap

1. To make the sauce, mix the Greek yogurt, garlic powder, dill weed, fresh lemon juice, grated cucumber, and a couple pinches of salt and pepper in a small bowl. Stir until combined. Set aside.

Tip

Wrap the grated cucumber in a clean kitchen towel. Squeeze the extra liquid out to avoid a soupy sandwich sauce.

Have an adult handy when you grate the cucumber. Cucumbers are wet and can make the grater slippery. Wrap a paper towel around the cucumber to help protect your fingers.

2. Set the pita on a cutting board and cut it in half. Spread the yogurt sauce evenly inside the 2 halves.

3. Slide 2 pieces of turkey, 1 slice of tomato, half the spinach, and 2 slices of cucumber into each pocket half.

4. Wrap the halves in plastic and refrigerate until ready to eat.

Variation Vegans and vegetarians can easily swap Greek yogurt with a vegan variety, and deli turkey for a non-meat selection. Try meatless chicken, tofu, or chickpeas. Falafel would be tasty too!

Burger Dippers

No need to fire up the grill or get out the buns! Just grab your favorite condiments and you can dip on the go. A new take on one of your favorite meals means you can bring burgers anywhere.

Prep time: 20 minutes • Cook time: 15 minutes • Makes 8 Dippers

Ingredients

½ pound ground beef or turkey

3 tablespoons bacon crumbles

2 tablespoons ranch dressing

¾ cup shredded cheddar cheese

¼ cup dill pickle chips, chopped

8-ounce (227-gram) package refrigerated crescent roll dough

ketchup and mustard, for dipping

Tools

large skillet

large baking sheet lined with parchment paper

spoon

measuring cups/spoons

spatula

1. Ask an adult to preheat the oven to 350 degrees.

2. Place a large skillet on the stove. Ask the adult to heat to medium-high. Add the ground beef to the skillet. Break the beef apart with a spoon as it cooks. It should be crumbly and browned all the way through after about 10 minutes.

3. Ask the adult to drain any grease from the meat. Stir in the bacon, ranch dressing, cheese, and pickles. Set aside.

4. Open the package of crescent dough. Roll it out onto a clean work surface, then pull the triangles apart. Place all the dough triangles on the baking sheet. Leave a few inches of space between each triangle.

5. Spoon the beef mixture evenly over each dough triangle. Then roll the triangles into crescents, starting with the shortest side.

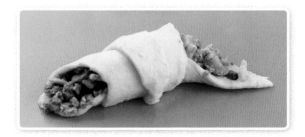

6. Place in the oven for 12 to 15 minutes, or until golden brown.

7. Serve hot, with dipping sauces.

   Variation Swap out the beef for 12 ounces (340 grams) chopped portabella mushrooms, any plant-based ground meat, or 1 ½ cups cooked beans.

Mac 'n Cheese Muffins

Mac and cheese is one of the most popular meals out there. But it doesn't always travel well. Make it to-go with these freezer-friendly cheesy pasta cups.

Prep time: 15 minutes • Cook time: 45 minutes • Makes about 12 muffins

Tip

To eat them later, wrap each cooked muffin in plastic wrap, place in a resealable bag, and then freeze. To reheat, place unwrapped muffins on a microwave-safe plate. Zap for 3 to 4 minutes or until warmed through.

Ingredients

2 tablespoons kosher salt

2 cups uncooked elbow macaroni

¼ cup panko bread crumbs

1 tablespoon olive oil

1 tablespoon butter

1 egg

1 cup milk

1 teaspoon mustard powder

1 teaspoon onion powder

2 cups shredded cheddar cheese, plus ½ cup for topping

4 ounces (113 grams) cream cheese, room temperature

garnish, such as fresh parsley, paprika, or grated Parmesan cheese

Tools

muffin tin lined with paper or silicone cupcake liners

large stockpot

measuring cups/spoons

stirring spoon

small bowl

fork

colander

1. Ask an adult to preheat oven to 350 degrees.

2. Fill a large stockpot with water. Add the salt. Ask the adult to bring the water to a boil. Then add the macaroni. Stir the water to keep the noodles from sticking. Cook for about 8 minutes.

3. While the pasta cooks, make your topping. Mix the panko bread crumbs with olive oil, and fluff with a fork until the crumbs are coated. Set aside.

4. When the pasta is cooked, ask the adult to drain it in the colander. Then return it to the pot.

5. Add the butter and egg to the pasta. Stir until coated. Pour in the milk, mustard powder, onion powder, cheddar cheese, and cream cheese. Stir until combined.

6. Scoop even portions of the macaroni mix into the muffin cups. Sprinkle with more cheese and the panko topping.

7. Place in the oven and bake for about 25 minutes.

8. Serve hot. Dust with fresh parsley, paprika, or grated Parmesan cheese.

Variation "Cheese" might be in the name, but vegans don't need to miss out on these marvelous muffins. Skip the butter, egg, milk, and cheeses in steps 5 and 6. Instead, add 1 cup of non-dairy plain milk, 2 teaspoons cornstarch, and ½ cup nutritional yeast. Sprinkle the muffins with vegan cheese and the panko mix, and you're ready to go.

Mini Chicken Pot Pies

Comfort food in bite-sized form!
These mini bites pack the same pot-pie punch as the full-sized versions.

Prep time: 15 minutes • Cook time: 25 minutes • Makes 10 mini pot pies

Ingredients

1 package refrigerated biscuit dough

10.5-ounce (300-gram) can cream of chicken soup

1 cup chopped cooked chicken

1 cup frozen peas and carrots

Tools

cutting board

rolling pin

muffin tin

medium bowl

stirring spoon

Tip

To save these for a meal on the go, place fully cooled pies on a baking sheet lined with parchment paper. Freeze for 4 hours. Once frozen, wrap each pie in plastic wrap. Store inside a resealable freezer bag in the freezer. To reheat, remove plastic wrap and place pot pie on a microwave-safe plate. Warm for 3 to 4 minutes until hot.

1. Ask an adult to preheat oven to 375 degrees.

2. Open the package of refrigerated biscuit dough. Separate the biscuits and turn them out onto a cutting board. Use the rolling pin to flatten each biscuit.

3. Place a biscuit in each muffin cup. Use your fingers to press the biscuit dough along the bottom and up the sides of the cup.

4. Mix the chicken soup, cooked chicken, and peas and carrots in a bowl. Spoon mixture evenly into each muffin cup.

5. Bake in the oven for 20 minutes or until the dough is golden brown. Let cool for 10 minutes before removing the mini pies.

Variation Make sure you check the labels of your refrigerated biscuit dough. Some common brands are already vegan!

Skip the chicken and use a meatless substitute. Then swap out the chicken soup with a homemade vegan-friendly creamy sauce. Saute 1 pound of chopped mushrooms in 2 tablespoons olive oil. Add 1 cup plain non-dairy milk such as soy, 2 tablespoons cornstarch, 1 teaspoon onion powder, and 1 teaspoon salt. Whisk and bring to a boil over medium-high heat. Reduce the heat to medium and cook for 5 minutes until the sauce thickens.

PB and J Protein Bars

Your favorite sandwich flavors can go beyond the bread! These treats are easy to make, don't need to be baked, and taste like the perfect PB & J. These snack bars are a great source of protein and energy.

Prep time: 10 minutes •
Cook time: 0 minutes (1 hour inactive) • Makes 8 bars

Ingredients

2 tablespoons butter

$^2/_3$ cup peanut butter

$^1/_3$ cup honey

$^1/_2$ teaspoon vanilla extract

2 cups old-fashioned rolled oats

$^1/_2$ cup peanut butter powder

$^1/_4$ teaspoon kosher salt

$^1/_3$ cup freeze-dried strawberries, plus extra for the top

$^1/_2$ cup strawberry jam

Tools

8-inch (20-cm) square baking dish

parchment paper

medium size microwave-safe bowl

measuring cups/spoons

spoon

cutting board

chef's knife

plastic wrap

1. Line the baking dish with parchment paper, letting some of the paper hang over the sides. This is so you can easily lift out the bars later.

2. In the microwave-safe bowl, melt the butter, peanut butter, and honey for 30 seconds. Stir. Repeat until the mixture is very warm and smooth, about 2 minutes.

3. Add the vanilla extract, oats, peanut butter powder, and salt. Stir well. The mixture will be sticky.

4. With an adult's help, chop the strawberries into bite-sized pieces and add them to the mixture.

5. Pour half the mixture into the baking dish. Use the bottom of a cup to firmly pack the bars into the dish. Spread strawberry jam over the bars and sprinkle the tops with crushed, freeze-dried strawberries.

6. Place in the refrigerator for 1 hour. Add the remaining bar mixture and refrigerate for another hour.

7. Use the parchment paper to lift the chilled bars out of the pan. With an adult's help, cut into 8 bars. Cover each in plastic wrap and return to the refrigerator. Eat within 7 days.

   Variation Nuts aren't necessary for this bar to be delicious! Replace the peanut butter and peanut butter powder with sunflower seed butter and sunflower seed protein powder for a nut-free delight!

23

Barbecue Snack Mix

Tangy, sweet, and smoky, this mix of crunchy crackers and nuts is saucy and sharp. Take these with you on the go, or fill a bowl for movie night at home.

Prep time: 10 minutes • Cook time: 1 hour • Makes 8 servings

Ingredients

2 cups toasted rice square-shaped cereal

2 cups corn square-shaped cereal

1 cup square pretzels

1 cup oyster crackers

1 cup peanuts

1 cup baked cheddar cheese crackers

½ cup barbecue sauce

2 tablespoons butter

1 ½ teaspoons dry barbecue rub

Tools

2 large baking sheets lined with parchment paper

large bowl

measuring cups/spoons

small microwave-safe bowl

spoon

spatula

paper towels

1. Ask an adult to preheat the oven to 250 degrees.

2. In a large bowl, combine the cereals, pretzels, oyster crackers, peanuts, and cheddar cheese crackers.

3. In a small microwave-safe bowl, combine the barbecue sauce, butter, and barbecue rub. Heat for 30 seconds in the microwave. Stir. Repeat until the mixture is smooth and the butter is completely melted.

4. Pour the barbecue sauce mix into the large bowl. Use a spatula to gently coat all the dry ingredients.

5. Spread the mixture out on the baking sheets. With the adult's help, bake for 45 minutes. Stir the mix on the sheet with a spatula every 15 minutes.

6. Remove from the oven. Ask the adult to transfer the hot mixture onto to a layer of paper towels. Let the mixture cool completely. Store in an airtight container or individual snack bags for up to 2 weeks.

Variation Most barbecue sauces are vegan, but check the label to be sure. Crackers, pretzels, and bagel chips are all interchangeable, so choose any combination of your favorite crunchy vegan treats. You can replace the butter in this recipe with buttery spread or vegetable oil.

Tropical Smoothie

Smooth, creamy, and dreamy—let a blender take you on an island retreat!
Thick and fruity, you'll be happy to slurp down this tasty smoothie. For breakfast,
dessert, or an in-between snack, this blended beverage
comes together in no time!

Prep time: 5 minutes • Cook time: 0 minutes • Makes 1 smoothie

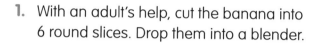

Ingredients

1 banana

4 ice cubes

½ cup orange juice

½ cup pineapple juice

6-ounce (170-gram) container
   vanilla yogurt

Tools

cutting board

knife

measuring cups/spoons

blender

1. With an adult's help, cut the banana into 6 round slices. Drop them into a blender.

2. Add the ice cubes, orange juice, pineapple juice, and yogurt.

3. Ask the adult to blend on high until the drink is smooth. Add more ice cubes if you prefer a thicker smoothie.

4. Serve in a glass and slurp immediately!

Variations There are many ways to change up a smoothie. Here are a few ideas.

Butter-Side-Up
1 tablespoon nut or sunflower butter

Tropical Threat
2 tablespoons full-fat coconut milk

Salad for Breakfast
handful of spinach
(you won't taste it, promise!)

Mixed-Up Mixture
swap out the fruit and juices in the recipe
for any you may prefer

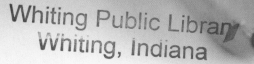

Banana Split
Pudding Parfait

Take your banana split, and . . . split? You can take a banana split on the go with this easy recipe. Store in the fridge, and grab one on the way out the door.

Prep time: 15 minutes • Cook time: 1 hour • Makes 4 pudding parfaits

Ingredients

3.4-ounce (96-gram) package instant vanilla pudding mix

2 cups cold milk

2 bananas, peeled and sliced

¼ cup pineapple chunks

4 strawberries, stems removed and cut into slices

canned whipped cream

4 tablespoons chocolate sauce

maraschino cherries

Tools

medium bowl

measuring cups/spoons

whisk

4 half-pint (250-mL) cups or jars

1. Whisk the pudding mix and milk together in a bowl. The pudding should start to set in 3 to 5 minutes.

2. Add ¼ cup of pudding to each cup.

3. Add a layer of bananas to each cup. Repeat with pineapple, and then strawberries.

4. Top the cups with a final layer of pudding.

5. Cover the cups tightly and place in the refrigerator for at least 1 hour.

6. To serve, add a squirt of whipped cream, a drizzle of chocolate sauce, and a cherry.

Variation Did you know most instant puddings are vegan? Make sure you check the label of yours to be sure. Instead of 2 cups of milk, use 1 cup of any non-dairy milk. Whisk for 2 minutes. Add another ½ cup and whisk another minute or 2. If it's too thick for your liking, add more milk a tablespoon at a time.

Cooking Glossary

flatbread (FLAT-bred)—a thin, wide bread

freeze-dry (FREEZ-DRY)—a technique for preserving food that removes all moisture

grate (GRAYT)—to turn a larger ingredient into small pieces by rubbing it on something rough, such as a grater

nutritional yeast (noo-TRISH-uh-uhl YEEST)—a form of yeast used as a vegan substitute in cooking

parchment paper (PARCH-muhnt PAY-puhr)—paper sold in rolls used for baking

parfait (par-FAY)—a dessert that contains distinct layers; layers may include fruit, yogurt, ice cream, whipped cream, cake, or syrup

pastry brush (PAY-stree BRUSH)—a cooking tool used to spread butter, oil, or glaze onto food

preheat (pre-HEET)—to heat an oven to a designated temperature before baking

protein (PROH-teen)—a substance found in foods such as meat, milk, eggs, and beans

rub (RUB)—a blend of seasonings typically rubbed on meat

whisk (WISK)—a wire kitchen tool used for mixing food

Tools

baking dishes

baking sheet

blender

chef's knife

cupcake liners

cutting board

grater

mason jars

measuring cups/spoons

standard muffin tin

nonstick skillet

parchment paper

pastry brush

pizza cutter

plastic wrap

rolling pin

spatulas

stockpot

whisk

Read More

My First Cookbook: Fun Recipes to Cook Together . . . With as Much Mixing, Rolling, Scrunching, and Squishing as Possible! Boston, MA: America's Test Kitchen, 2020.

O'Driscoll, Lisa. *Roll It, Slice It, Mash It, Dice It!: Over 75 Super Yummy Recipes for Kids.* New York: Castle Point Books, 2021.

Spears, Anthony. *Chef Junior: A Real Food Guide to Learning How To Cook—By Kids For Kids.* New York: Sterling Publishing Co., Inc., 2020.

Internet Sites

Cooking With Kids
https://cookingwithkids.org/

Food Network: Cooking With Kids
https://www.foodnetwork.com/recipes/packages/recipes-for-kids/cooking-with-kids

The Spruce Eats: 12 Cooking Basics Everyone Should Know
https://www.thespruceeats.com/cooking-basics-for-everyone-4684010